I DIEI

I Died, I Am Dead, I Die

Cornelius Wambi Gulere

Published by Beads of Love Ministry, 2025.

I DIED, I AM DEAD, I DIE

First edition. February 14, 2025.

ISBN: 979-8230452362

Written by Cornelius Wambi Gulere.

Also by Cornelius Wambi Gulere

I Died, I Am Dead, I Die
The Narrow Gate: Nature's Storms
The Human Brain

Watch for more at https://www.facebook.com/
cornelius.wambigulere.1.

Table of Contents

The Banquet and the Binding 1
Fasting in the Dark 4
Midnight Truths 8
A Life Delayed 10
The Use That Death Has for Life 12
Riddle #034757# 14
A Traveler's Gratitude 20
Silence, Shouted 23
Dry, Dead, Dumb 25
Menses in Old Age 27
A Short Life Spun Long 30
Miles Through Smiles 36
I Died, I Am Dead, I Die 39
Grey Before Time 43
Forgive Me, A Sinner 46
Breath of Song 50
Santa's Secret Night 52
Heartful Community Life 55
A Cry Across the Distance 58
Beads of Love 61
Wandering Call 64
Silent Cross 67
Paths We Choose 70
Weaving of Two Threads 73
Threads of the Human Text 76
Matron of Many Paths 79
The Unseen Pillar 82
The Spectacles Found 85
Allegory of Two the Mothers 88
Light on the Stand 90
Voices in the Forest 92

The Journey Ahead 95
The Greek Wall 98
The Word to Loosen: Λύω 101
Depth of Aorist Forms 111
War in the Middle East 114
City on a Hill 117
Warning Flame 120
Shelter of Hope 123
Keys, Doors, and Shutters 126
Thornbush Rhapsody 129
Tale of Shadows and Sparks 132

To You Who Is

On this Way Is

At the marketplace,where voices rise and deals are made,he agreed to sponsor my funeral—if I could buy him a puppy.Easier said than done,but I did it.

The Banquet and the Binding

I was called from the roadside,
plucked from dust and wandering feet,
led into the banquet hall—
your feast laid before me,
your voice in the air,
your hands stretched in welcome.

Yet, O Lord, you saw me—
unworthy.
My garments were torn with pride,
stained with the lust of my own calling,
and you ordered the stewards,
"Bind him, cast him out,
where the night is cold,
where teeth gnash in the silence of regret."

I answered your call,
I heeded the voices sent to summon me,
yet here I stand—
a guest, a stranger,
a shadow among the light-bearers.

What then shall I do
but love and let go?
To walk in the light,

reject the false allure of the world,
forsake the fleeting glories
that shine only for men,
and turn instead
to You, the Father of Light.

My pride, my hunger to be *your own called*,
lay them aside,
that I may anoint your body
through the broken hands of my neighbor,
whom I will not always have.

That pot of oil—
not for my shelves,
not for my vanity,
but for the homeless poor at my door,
for the one whose eyes beg a lift
while I cruise past in haste,
shopping endlessly for things
I will never consume.

Break this alabaster jar!
Let the fragrance rise—
not for my comfort,
but for my foe,
who in my false sight
was never worthy to be anointed.

As a child, forgive me.
For I am strong, yet weary,
like an old rug that knows all corners well.
I have stumbled at your coming,

hesitated at your knock.
I have loved to hate
as much as I hated to love.

Yet you renewed me in your baptism,
saying—
"While you hate your brother,
the unseen, the ignored,
you hate me,
and so you will stumble still,
even while keeping the law."

Save, O Lord, your people,
and bless your inheritance.
Take me not from your feast,
but teach me to be clothed in love,
that I may walk in light
and sit at your table forever.

Amen.

Fasting in the Dark

I woke from a nap,
refreshed yet restless,
a day of toil behind me,
a fast ahead—
anxiety swelled like hunger,
the fear of emptiness
leading to fullness.

I stuffed my body,
storing food like treasure,
gorging in selfish haste,
knowing and unknowing,
then lay down,
a python coiled,
digesting the day's catch.

Soft music soothed,
hard floor held me,
as my belly worked
while my mind wandered.
How long will this take?

A day, a week,
the fifty days of the Great Fast?
Through Triodion to the Lord's Day,

through Pentecost,
one hundred days—
a century stretching ahead.

Yes, the light shines,
and I see the darkness
in my ways,
the idol I have worshipped:
food.
Nourishing the body,
weakening the spirit.
A hunger that is more than hunger,
an appetite laced with fear—
unseen, unknown, unnecessary.

Can I heal myself by food alone?
Or do I serve two masters,
risking the loss of both?

These eyes,
gourmet, greedy,
this mouth,
quick to break the fast,
this hand,
swift to take,
this tongue,
too eager to taste—
who is to blame?

Not me, I say.
It is this eye, this mouth,
this head, this hand,

this tongue, these feet—
Lord, You gave them to me.
I do not, I did not, I will not—
yet always, I do.
I did.
And I will.

Falling, failing,
feeding with the pigs,
breaking the fast on sweetness above,
while another, below,
feasts on grass for grace.

I am no longer worthy
to be called sun,
nor moon,
nor star.
I am darkness,
spread wide upon the world.

Where I stand or fall,
it makes no difference—
no light comes from dark diets,
until I learn to shut my mouth,
close my craving eyes,
still my restless hands,
silence my wandering feet.

That the Sun,
rising in each microsecond,
in every passing day,
will burn away my weakness,

and make me whole.

Midnight Truths

I prosper, I give,
I pour out my all,
to the one who labors not,
yet takes it all.

Words—spoken, done, kept—
molded me, moved me,
or did they?
Was I called, or coerced?
Led, or deceived?

Why do they have
as much more as I have not?
To whom much is given,
even more shall be stacked,
while the empty-handed
learn lack upon lack.

Sick, unhealthy,
the body wilts before its time.
Menopause—why not?
Why not sell it all,
give it all,
follow the poor into the dust
and be free?

Yet the ones who shine,
flamboyant in spirit and wealth,
have unmasked the riddles.
Now I see:
Start and prosper.
Stop and die poor
in the truth that never fed a mouth.

It is midnight,
and I must rise.
Dreams, dreams, dreams—
shadows on my walls,
whispers in my bones.

And still, I go.

A Life Delayed

My life has been delayed.
By the time I arrive,
the doors have already closed.

Jobs, degrees, dreams—
for the young,
for the under-30s,
for those whose clocks
ticked on time.

At 31, I wait—
for the next stage, the next opening.
A second degree at 40—too late.
A PhD at 41—too old.
Postdoc at 51?
No, only for the "early career,"
for those younger than 45.

By the time universities
call for career professors at 50,
I am neither young nor senior,
just aged without place,
an elder without a seat at the table.

Age anxiety rules.
What do I do
when the world measures worth
by the speed of arrival?
When those in power
cling until death,
shifting goalposts,
barring the way?

I watch grandfathers
become childlike again,
starting life anew
as elders who never leave.
Muzeeyi—
a name that grants honor,
yet denies opportunity.

Language laces into the flesh—
words twist and shape fate.
What does it mean
to bear the name elder
when it only builds walls?
Must I change my name
to gain access,
to find my chance,
to carve a path
where the road was closed?

Africans smile,
but at what cost?
A lifetime.

The Use That Death Has for Life

I lived on after I had gone,
lower in breath but bolder in absence.
Why does man feel most alive in death,
yet in life, he is left to struggle?

Now I see—
the use that death has for life.
What would life know,
if death did not remind it
of what it means to be?

Does death be?
Like life becomes,
lighting the way of being,
what can death do
but step outside of being,
leaving echoes behind?

I remember—
the many who came, hands wide,
to greet my child,
born on a weekend, a gift of joy.
Yet when my elder bowed on Wednesday,
the city stopped,
its breath held, its doors closed,

12

to let the elder pass.

Death is part of the party,
woven into our words:

Omugenzi—one who is going.

Omufu—the silent departed.

Omulambo—the weight left behind.

Names that move,
that whisper of a journey,
not an end.

And we who stay?
Are we late?
Later?
Or merely waiting
as our platters are plated
for another day?

Riddle #034757#

This riddle is being performed through the Seven Steps Lens of the Gulere 2016 Theory of the Riddle Performance that in brief states that the true riddle has seven interpolated steps: Antecedent, Precedent, Unravelling, Crowning, Declamation, Affirmation and Agreement. The Lusoga language term "Kikoiko" rendered in English as "riddle" is literary "It is What it is" meaning that a riddle though it may be fiction but it is fact as performed. It cannot be fixed as it grows and dies too.

Step 1 – Antecedent
(The Opening of the Riddle)
Kikoiko! – The riddle is spoken.
It is what it is!
A question posed, yet already answered.
A veil drawn, waiting to be lifted.
Kiidhe! – Let it come.
It is what it is!
A sequence of numbers:
0, 3, 4, 7, 5, 7.
Do you hear their rhythm?
Do you see their meaning?
What do they tell of time, of fate, of life?

Step 2 – Precedent
(The Groundwork for Unraveling)
Not all riddles beg an answer.

Some demand reason.
Some require history.
Some whisper in tongues unknown,
yet are familiar to the heart.

Lusoga is a beautiful language,
as is Greek, as is English, as is all tongues.
Yet what is "riddle" in your language?
Is it Greek to me, or am I lost
in the echoes of what words hide
and what numbers reveal?

0 – Ex nihilo? Perhaps.
But I was 9/12 when I became 1/12.
Another Kikoiko for another day.
For now—Mpirya? No, not the case.
It is what it is!

Step 3 – Unraveling
(The Untying of the Knot)
Let the numbers speak:
0 – Nothing? Or everything before it began?
3 – The Trinity? Marriage? A binding of souls?
4 – A child, a turning, a new direction.
7 – Completion, prophecy, fullness of time.
5 – A break, a departure, a wandering.
7 – A return, a renewal, a future unfolding.
Kikoiko, kiidhe! It is What it is!
Do you hear it?
A tale told,
not in words,
but in life lived, numbered, spoken

through the rhythm of time.

Step 4 – Crowning
(The Chief, The Prize, The Honor Bestowed)
Who wears the crown of this riddle?
Who is the chief? Give me the Chief!
Mpa Omwami!
None other than
His Beatitude Anastasios of Albania—
a name of light,
a mission of fire,
a father to orphans,
a beacon to lost lands.

Born in Greece, sent to Africa,

Albania, a snake among wolves,
a stranger among strangers,
yet made one with them.
He walked in the dust,
preached to the forgotten,
built churches where ruins stood.

A missionary, a scholar, an archbishop—
a bridge between histories,
a living flame that burned
where darkness once reigned.

To him, the crown of this riddle belongs.

Step 5 – Declamation

(The Cry of the Riddler to His Chief)
And I stand before him,
Gulere Cornelius, son of Wambi and Perepetua,
of Nsinze, a land where he, you, walked
before I could walk.

Your Beatitude,
you loved me before I knew myself.
You visited my people before I could speak.
You embraced my village before I knew its name.

And when I came to you,
when I sought your blessing in Tirana,
you gave it freely,
you sent me forth to lead,
but the world did not welcome the poor.

I was cast out,
not by you,
but by a world that weighs men in silver,
measures worth by gold.

Syndesmos crumbled under my poverty,
and I, a man without a place,
stood in the shadow of a mission denied.

So now, I call to you,
"Your Beatitude, come for me.
Take me where I may serve.
Make me a missionary,
as you were made a missionary.

Let me walk the road you walked,
for here, I have no writ to do so."

Step 6 – Affirmation
(The Meaning Laid Bare for Debate and Reasoning)
What then is 0, 3, 4, 7, 5, 7?
Not just numbers,
but a map, a prophecy, a life.

0 – A life that was nothing.
3 – Three years a deacon, a servant's call.
4 – Four years a presbyter, an elder's burden.
7 – Seven years of service, of prophecy, of endurance.
5 – Five lived decades of struggle, of longing, of seeking.
7 – Seven years beyond life, shaping a future still unwritten.

By the Ides of March,
I will stand at #034757 years
of life shaped in service,
of time woven into meaning.

Is this not beautiful?
Is this not the tale of a soul numbered?
Kikoiko—it is what it is!

Step 7 – Agreement
(The Final Concession, the Sealing of the Riddle)
Do you concede defeat?
Not in loss, but in learning.
Do you see the path as I have walked it?

You did not know
that time could be counted this way.
You did not know
that numbers could tell a tale
of faith, of struggle, of calling.

Kikoiko! Kiidhe!
It is what it is.
And the riddle is answered,
not in words,
but in the life it reflects.

Happy birthday, Mwalimu Bukenya!
So tell me, traveler,
will you walk this path with me?
For another Kikoiko waits,
another journey to unfold.

And so we go—
as we always have,
as we always will.

A Traveler's Gratitude

I thank you—
for your kindness,
for your love,
for holding me up
on this day of reckoning.

This weight upon my head,
this burden on my journey,
I do not know
how to carry alone.
Without your hand,
without your shoulder,
I would not have taken
even a single step.

The Archon,
Leadership 100,
the selection committee,
the heads of departments,
the RAs,
and all of you,
my fellow travelers—
you have filled my purse,
set my ticket in hand.
Bills paid.

The road is clear.
I can move forward,
back and forth,
because you have chosen me
as your own.

I serve you,
and you serve me the more.
I give what I have freely received,
and you give
what you have earned
through labor and sweat.
I thank you.

You—
who have lent your ear,
your eye,
your voice,
your mind,
your hand,
your foot—
to remove the log from my eye,
to temper my soul,
so that I may serve
and find peace
where I now live as home,
and where home once lived
before the five and the seven
since my nativity.
Mother, father, brothers,
village entire,
Syndesmos,

the Church.

April 1969—
called to new birth.
November 3, 2002—
matrimony sealed.
January 17, 2018—
reborn in death.
February 28, 2021—
affirmed in life.

To be who I am,
grateful to be—
a father,
kasisi,
pater.
What does this mean?

I thank you.
You have given,
that I may remain true
to my calling,
to be a proud father
in all that is good and pure.
And woe to me—
if I become
a hindrance
to the Good News
of Him who comes
in the Name of the Lord.

Silence, Shouted

Why do you never shut up?
Who told you we needed your woes?
The mind of divorce thinks this,
pities the spouse
who endures endless chattering,
a silence lost before it's found.

Silence—silencer—silenced.
Slice the voice from the mouth,
watch it wilt,
but does silence make truth less real?
Does a dumb friend, nodding, shaking,
make less noise than a storm?

See.
Hear.
Touch.
Smell.
Feel from within—
but no eye has seen, no ear has heard?
Is that so?

The tongue curls with flavors unspoken,
words unsaid, salted on the lips,
a whisper melting

into the ear waiting,
near the clear dear-done-dance.

A therapy of silence
is not what the wind winds
in this noisy life.
Not that I crave the clamour,
but the heart,
in the heat of fear,
faints at freedom.

And in that faint,
what else is left but to shout—
I am done with you.
I need to go
and make hurt grin.

Dry, Dead, Dumb

I have no time to become—
no space to stretch into girlhood,
no curve of breast, no crimson flow,
no flutter of something soft and new.

I was born aged, skin wrapped in sorrow,
a child only in years, but never in feeling.
At thirteen, I carry the weight of ancestors,
their eyes in mine, their grief in my hands.

War wove itself into my body,
threaded loss through my veins.
Before my feet could bruise on stones,
my womb withered, dust settled deep—
not barren, not sterile, not aborted,
but emptied by mourning before it could be full.

Motherhood died before its death,
not by plague, not by blade,
but by the echoing silence of too many funerals.
I bleed grief instead of life,
carry shadows instead of sons.
And in this silence, men turn to men,
women to women, lost in their own reflection—
seeking warmth where blood once called.

My brother? I do not know when last
his seed knew air,
for the cycles that once answered him
have vanished into dust.

No history, no time, no crime, no prime—
just dry, dead, dumb,
and the wind whispers of what was,
but never will be again.

Menses in Old Age

My body breathes, finally,
exhaling what it held too long.
Blood, late but not lost,
flows through years of silence.
Too much work, too little rest,
no births, no takes—
only the coming and going of water,
changed but the same.

Not like my mother,
nor hers before,
and my brother—
he says the same.

The pain, the pus, the pee, the pot,
all diseased, all burdened
by what I endured,
by what was done
or what I did not do—
as a child, as a girl, as a woman.

Who? they ask.
Not cursed.
Not a dog knocking me.
Not witches or craft,

but me—
not minding my mind,
not guarding my heart.

And now, at 65 and 62,
I am 26 and 56,
young and old,
beginning where the end once stood.

How do I speak this in my tongue?
"I knocked my toe?"
Again, Granny's tale spills into the street,
eyes pause,
lips part—
Is she well?

Luckily, not crimson.
Reddish-purple dress—
it hides what only she knows,
what only she feels
as it happens inside her life.
You who sees,
see better.
When I wear the thick wig,
when I paint my lips bold,
when I go to parties and funerals alike—
know that I am searching,
that I am lost,
that I am hoping.

If trauma would wane,
if time would heal,

I would be natural again.
And when that happens—
you will know.

A Short Life Spun Long

Swollen feet,
ankles thick with time,
eyes dimming,
fingers fainting—
this is what it means
to be technologically able?

Who would dare say
working from home
is a diseased decision,
when the disease
gets its reward?

Each family
bought a computer,
a phone for every child,
every worker—
a new norm,
a trendy trap.

Stay home,
fewer cars, fewer crowds—
as long as the internet flows,
as long as power hums,
as long as food arrives,

as long as screens
keep us breathing.

What the bitter tree cures
in a second at no cost,
life is lost
where ICUs fail
to unburden lungs
drowning in air.

And now—
water pools in my eyes,
my belly, my legs,
while I sit for long hours,
working from home,
afraid to breathe
what is outside my door.
What a strategy.

Three handsets,
four desktops,
all connected
to the world—
so I never have to leave.

I reach across seas,
beyond borders,
without ever stepping out.

This is terrific.
This is tragic.

I enjoy the long,
unpaid hours,
cheaper for all,
except for me—
the hours stretch,
the life shortens,
spun thin and promised long.

Where I Stand Now

Where I stand now,
the sun shines as it did yesterday,
bright, majestic, unwavering—
a constant king,
inconsiderate of who stands beneath
its striking fluorescent rays.

Sometimes a rainbow forms between,

clouds weave shade to temper might,
soft hands cooling summer's height,
winter's bite, spring's bloom, autumn's sigh—
but still, it is the same,
yesterday, today, tomorrow.

No hurry, no delay,
no west nor east,
north nor south,
center nor periphery.
I strike—soft, slight,
hard or harder,
but to all, in all,
at all times, the same.

Love, beauty, joy, kindness,
patience keeping time,
yet holding none.
Every hour counted
in eternity's unbroken song.

Only I and thee,
with whom I serve,
see differences.
Under the sun,
shadows stretch
from shrubs and towering trees,
canopies dense,
populations unmatched.

Some numerous,
some thickets,

some encroached,
lamenting their loss,
diminishing before time.
Some stand strong,
feeding on the sun's strength,
fruitful, never resting.
Others, dormant—
rocks of ages,
unmoved but cracked,
worn thin by the abrasion of time.

Yet, I sing my song
and take the sun as mine,
no matter where I stand,
sit, or lie.
For the sun comes for me,
and though my branches bear no fruit,
I still share its light.

And Thee—
who rocks the world,
who gives power to shine,
says none may claim
to have no right to be.

For if you stand,
sit, or lie beneath this light,
you have the write—the right—
to receive and to give.

Where I stand now,
I write.

I digest.
I bathe in light—
not the sun of this world,
but the Sun that fills the world
with the power to be.

To Thine be the glory.

Miles Through Smiles

Smile—by nature,
not by force,
not a mask made to hide the gloom.

Would the baby boy,
born bright,
becoming man,
becoming grandman,
smile as broad and brilliant
as the baby girl,
grown strong,
breasts beating in rhythm,
proud to say,
See this—see what it says about me?

Yet see—
how disease has traced its lines,
how cancer crept where life once thrived,
dulling the glow,
silencing the embrace.

See this grandmother lament—
her bras carry acidified burdens,
woven poisons pressing soft flesh,
turning milk to stone,

turning bloom to wither.
The boob boomed by sickness,
the smile faded,
the face now a façade
of joy lost to war inside the skin.

Did we not say food is fresh,
that blood and milk flow
from the earth's goodness?
Did we not say—
Eat well, and love will stretch for miles,
smiles will bloom,
and youth will live natural lives?

Forty years wandering in deserts,
forty days fasting in the wilderness,
forty days waiting, watching—
all measuring the road
to the promised land.

When shall normalization come?
Will the smiles return?
Or is there blockage, tightness,
a broken pot,
lungs gasping for airless air—
so thin, so strained,
that the body must leave,
seeking a place
where breath is full again?

I was made
to see miles through smiles,

to know life by the joy it carries.

But when will my maturation come?
I ask my greatest teacher,
I open the greatest book.

What does it say?

I Died, I Am Dead, I Die

I am long dead—seven years.
What is this to you?

At the marketplace,
where voices rise and deals are made,
he agreed to sponsor my funeral—
if I could buy him a puppy.
Easier said than done,
but I did it.

And so, on 17 January 2018,
they laid me down,
resting with the saints,
from reader to deacon,
to serve at the Holy Altar.
Buried with Him
that I may resurrect with Him.

That one—
like Jonah fleeing Nineveh,
first rejecting,
then accepting,
officiated my funeral.
Unworthy though I was.
The world is sweet,

and to leave it willingly—
not easy.
Even on my way to Golgotha,
buying sweet bananas,
a nail from the market shade
pierced my shirt.
A warning—
How can you think of food
when death is at hand?

But what of my wife,
my children?
Shall they go hungry
because I am gone?
My mother, my siblings,
my friends,
all there,
pinching dust onto dust,
as I became dust.

Yet new funeral clothes—
black robes, green,
sometimes white, sometimes purple,
but always black—
covered all wear and tear.

"He will tire of it," they said.
"He will return to suits and neckties."
Return?
Come back as a spirit to haunt us?

The wind, the sun, the hurricane—

hunger, and worst of all,
the COVID,
shaking graves,
taking lives,
until one was taken away
and I was elevated,
to serve in the graveyard,
inside,
like the first among the dead.

And there—right there—
the Prodigal Son returns.
"I am not worthy to be called your son."

Three years later,
then four,
the elevation deepens,
dying even more
in the same body,
soul taken up,
awaiting judgment day.

I died.
I am dead.
I die.

That they may live.
Live to the full.

I, a Fool for Christ,
file my gratitude

from this side of Life,
from the outside of the world.

Grey Before Time

I like my head and chin grey,
silver threads woven before their time.
It came faster than I expected—
half my father's age,
his hair still black,
mine turning to mist.
What does this mean?

I wish to be young,
to feel young,
to act young,
to enter my final rest young.
But he—he loves to be Muzeeyi,
the Old Man,
a title now given at birth,
a clan name,
a family name.

How will the daughter-in-law
call the name of her father-in-law
now given to her firstborn son?
Politeness demands a veil,
a whisper in place of a word,
and so Muzeeyi becomes his name.

Or perhaps, for those
who take a foreign name,
his is abandoned entirely
out of respect—is it?

Does respect erase
those it is meant to honor?
Or does it raise them higher,
stretch their years longer?

Colourful silence,
smiling noisily—
is that the colonial nature of things?
Mushrooms thrive
where they colonize,
silent invaders taking root.
Is the sin of such a place
not an old one?

My name,
my mane,
my minor,
my mine—
the well from which
I draw my all.
I do not age
by name or status,
not by looks or likes,
but by the mood inside me,
by the weight of things around me.

Do not stop me

from mourning my dead,
from celebrating my life.

Let me grieve,
let me live,
let me wear my grey
as I please.

Forgive Me, A Sinner

I sought forgiveness,
to each and every soul—
known and unknown,
sinned against knowingly
and unknowingly.
As I forgive,
so do I seek to be forgiven,
a prayer as daily bread.

Yet one asks—
What sin?
For what do you ask forgiveness?
I do not know.

Must I explain myself?
Do I love sinfully,
or am I merely tempered
by remembrances of wrongs?
Then why ask *what*—
when love seeks
and love gives
without measure,
without question?
The door is opened
to the prodigal son,

yet look at his brother,
look what he thinks,
what he says,
what he does—
to his father,
to his brother,
to himself above all.

I am unworthy,
says the tax collector.
The high and mighty
Pharisee asks,
What wrong have you done?
Can you elaborate?
Then I can forgive.

Is this confession?
Must I confess
with my mouth
to be forgiven,
or with my heart?

Which is the way,
the truth,
the life?
To ask is not to contest.
But if I do not speak,
how will they know
that I am repentant?
Yet—
who needs to know?
Isn't my Listener

able to hear
in silence?
To be present
even in the void,
where space itself
is filled with power?

I am sorry carries weight.
Forgive me carries even more.
I forgive you is weightier still,
and mightier,
for in this,
the Sun shines bright.

Heavyweight boxing
is not about the gloves,
but the moves—
so we must move
as sons of light
while we still have the light.

Here or there,
I do not ask when,
how,
what,
why,
as the world does.
I ask only this—
forgive me, a sinner.

For I know only
the weight of my sins,

though their magnitude
escapes me.
Yet in my bones,
I feel their ache,
deep in my marrow—
diseased,
corrupt,
infidel,
adulterous,
consumptive,
tempered by ill temperance,
by fear,
by counterfeit love
that binds me to mud,
to hate,
to shame,
to anxiety.

Holding onto
what is not mine,
even withholding
what is mine
from those
who are my own.

And before I cry,
Lord, have mercy,
I seek mercy
from my own
of my own.

Breath of Song

Today, my voice found its healer,
Wilcox—singer, dancer, actor—
but to me, a teacher, a guide,
a tuner of breath and tone.

She diagnosed my song's ailments,
breath too short,
voice too hoarse,
failing to lift the hymn
to the Panagia,
the Mother of Light.

How could I magnify her
with a voice dark and weak?
Yet today, I learned—
to breathe,
to pace,
to sing in rhythm,
like sipping thick yogurt
through a straw.

My chest, expanding—
lungs out, back and front,
grounded, poised,
not lifting high in strain,

nor sinking low in despair.
Paws three, ready to pounce,
balancing breath like prayer.

And now, in *Lusoga*,

the hymn soars clearer:

"*Ighe atenderezebwa okusinga Bakerubim,*

atagerageranhizika era agulumizibwa okuwula Baseraphim,
ighe inhe Kibbumba tukugulumiza."

More honorable than the Cherubim,
higher than the Seraphim,
in breath and song,
we magnify her.

At 56, I have learned to breathe,
to let my voice rise
as incense in the air,
as a waltz in harmony.

And for this, I leave the theatre glad.

Santa's Secret Night

(11/08/2024)

On a chilly eve where joy was the spark,
We gathered close as the skies turned dark.
Secret Santa, a tale so sweet,
Where laughter and mystery were set to meet.

No scampering through bushes for gifts to find,
Nor Christmas trees with treasures entwined.
But hearts were light, and spirits were high,
As laughter danced beneath the night sky.

◈ (Chorus)
Oh, the gift of love, the gift of cheer,
A secret shared, a bond so near.
In laughter and kindness, we take delight,
On Secret Santa's magical night. ◈

Like St. Nicholas, the secret we'd keep,
As names were whispered, promises deep.
"Guess who gave?" came the playful jest,
And if they failed, the giver confessed.

With words of warmth and wishes true,

We shared our hearts, old bonds renewed.
No riches required, just moments so dear,
The spirit of Christmas made perfectly clear.

◈ **(Chorus)**
Oh, the gift of love, the gift of cheer,
A secret shared, a bond so near.
In laughter and kindness, we take delight,
On Secret Santa's magical night. ◈

Not all received a trinket or prize,
But no one left with downcast eyes.
For joy itself became the gift,
A treasure eternal, spirits to lift.

Yet lessons linger, in the heart's own hue,
What does gifting mean? What is truly due?
Is it the box, the bow, the glitter and gold,
Or the warmth of a story shared and told?

◈ **(Bridge)**
O Lord, remind us in this festive air,
To give with love and tender care.
For gifts of the soul outshine the rest,
In the heart of the giver, we're truly blessed. ◈

So let us lament the times we forgot,
The essence of giving is love, not a lot.
No greater gift than a smile or embrace,
A moment of kindness, a touch of grace.

◈ (**Final Chorus**)
Oh, the gift of love, the gift of cheer,
A secret shared, a bond so near.
In laughter and kindness, we take delight,
On Secret Santa's magical night. ◈

On this Orthodox Christmas, let us sing,
Of the joy and love such nights can bring.
For whether Christian or of another creed,
In giving and laughter, we're all agreed.

◈ (**Outro**)
So here's to the spirit, the laughter, the light,
Of Secret Santa's wondrous night.
May hearts be full, may kindness flow,
In this sacred season, let it grow. ◈

Heartful Community Life

In the warmth of the Church, a light we found,
A place where grace and love abound.
We knelt in prayer, for all, for each,
The sick, the frail, the hearts to reach.

◇ (Chorus)
Open hearts and minds so clear,
Love's embrace draws us near.
In every soul, a spark divine,
Through parish life, God's blessings shine. ◇

For children's laughter, gifts we shared,
A sign of love that showed we cared.
The elders smiled, their burdens eased,
In such small acts, our Lord is pleased.

A common meal, a table wide,
With no division, none cast aside.
For in this feast, His presence dwells,
A taste of heaven, where joy compels.
◇ (Chorus)
Open hearts and minds so clear,
Love's embrace draws us near.
In every soul, a spark divine,
Through parish life, God's blessings shine. ◇

We spoke of dreams, of what could be,
Of building a stronger community.
To mend what's broken, to lift what's low,
To guide each other in love's gentle flow.

To visit the sick, the lost, the forlorn,
To carry their burdens, their spirits reborn.
A bent back healed, a soul set free,
For Christ knows all, our infirmity.

◇ (Bridge)
O Lord, You see what we do not,
The hidden wounds, the battles fought.
Your healing hand, Your mercy flows,
To all who seek, Your love bestows. ◇

Community life, a path so sweet,
Where hearts and hands together meet.
An open heart, a bridge of grace,
A refuge found in this holy space.

Encouragement offered, hope renewed,
Through simple acts, our faith is proved.
A smile, a word, a hand to hold,
In love's own language, truth is told.

◇ (Chorus)
Open hearts and minds so clear,
Love's embrace draws us near.
In every soul, a spark divine,

Through parish life, God's blessings shine. ◈

Let us be watchful, let us be kind,
To the needs of others, both body and mind.
For many are sick and do not know,
But Christ in His mercy bids us grow.

◈ (**Final Chorus**)
Open hearts and minds so clear,
Love's embrace draws us near.
In every soul, a spark divine,
Through parish life, God's blessings shine. ◈

So sing this song in joy and peace,
Let every burden find release.
For in parish life, God's light we see,
A glimpse of His eternal harmony.

◈ (**Outro**)
May our lives be bridges, strong and wide,
To carry the world on love's great tide.
Through parish life, His kingdom comes,
In every heart, His will is done. ◈

A Cry Across the Distance

We missed the call, our voices fell,
Into the chasm where silence dwells.
Time zones tangled, lives apart,
A family's bond stretched at the heart.

The saying rings, so often true,
"A family that prays together stays through."
But here and there, scattered wide,
The head calls out, yet limbs divide.

◇ (Chorus)
Oh, the miles are long, the silence deep,
But love's a river, strong to keep.
In prayers unspoken, our spirits meet,
In God's great mercy, the bond's complete. ◇

Each in their state, each path their own,
Bearing burdens, often alone.
Yet love endures, unconditioned, pure,
Through trials faced, through wounds obscure.
A coffee shared, a word of care,
A moment stolen, a silent prayer.
Embraces fleeting, yet deeply known,
A seed of hope in hearts is sown.

◇ (**Chorus**)
Oh, the miles are long, the silence deep,
But love's a river, strong to keep.
In prayers unspoken, our spirits meet,
In God's great mercy, the bond's complete. ◇

For mothers toil, for daughters yearn,
Sons like fathers, their lessons learn.
Yet each grows weary, each soul bereft,
In a world of struggle, some dreams are left.

But hold, dear friend, though hope seems thin,
The dawn will break, the light will win.
A time will come, beyond the strife,
When family binds not just in life.

◇ (**Bridge**)
O Lord, who sees the unseen pain,
Bind us together, make us whole again.
Through unspoken love, through silent tears,
We wait in faith, we wait through years. ◇

The Ides of March will someday bring,
A reckoning vast, a healing spring.
Where unity rises, surpassing the self,
And family treasures its truest wealth.

Until that time, we hold and wait,
Through fleeting moments, through shifting fate.
A prayer for you, a prayer for me,
A love unbroken, eternally free.

◇ (**Final Chorus**)
Oh, the miles are long, the silence deep,
But love's a river, strong to keep.
In prayers unspoken, our spirits meet,
In God's great mercy, the bond's complete. ◇

So let us embrace, in faith abide,
Though scattered, love shall be our guide.
A family whole, when time aligns,
In God's great plan, His holy design.

◇ (**Outro**)
Across the distance, near or far,
We're bound together, as we are.
For in His love, we always stay,
A family strong, come what may. ◇

Beads of Love

A Song of Gratitude and Hope

On the sixth of December, the spark was lit,
A bead of love, from hands so fit.
Women crafting with tender care,
Each bead a story, a love to share.

For children who toil, their dreams on hold,
These treasures transform their lives untold.
With paper designs and hands so true,
Hope is woven, dreams renew.

◈ **(Chorus)**
Freely received, freely give,
In the spirit of love, we help others live.
Beads of love, a shining chain,
Binding hearts through joy and pain. ◈

From **AS**, the seeds of kindness grew,
A guiding light in all we do.
TJ brought courage, a voice so clear,
Whispering hope to those who hear.

AD laid plans, with wisdom's grace,

Helping the project find its place.
And **EB**, a spark of giving bright,
Turned darkened paths to beams of light.

◈ **(Chorus)**
Freely received, freely give,
In the spirit of love, we help others live.
Beads of love, a shining chain,
Binding hearts through joy and pain. ◈

GB inspired, spreading the call,
For every giver, no matter how small.
EC gave heart, with hands so skilled,
Dreams of children soon fulfilled.

GF wove words, a storyteller's art,
Uniting the many, heart to heart.
While **IT** brought strength, a quiet might,
Steady hands turning wrongs to right.

◈ **(Bridge)**
O Trinity of wonders, guide us still,
With love unending, shape our will.
The Father gives, the Son redeems,
The Spirit sustains our brightest dreams. ◈

NF spread the word with fervent zeal,
Helping others the impact feel.
Together we stand, each role a thread,
In the Textile of love, where no tear is shed.

Three days of giving, three months of school,
What wonders arise when love is the rule.
To gift, to share, to take and tell,
Is to echo the voice of Emmanuel.

◇ (**Chorus**)
Freely received, freely give,
In the spirit of love, we help others live.
Beads of love, a shining chain,
Binding hearts through joy and pain. ◇

So let us give, with hearts aglow,
That every child may learn and grow.
In the unmercenary spirit, let love be the guide,
For in every bead, God's grace resides.

◇ (**Outro**)
Beads of love, from hand to hand,
A chain unbroken, across the land.
Together we weave a future bright,
In faith, in hope, in love's pure light. ◇

We are grateful for all your gifts.

Wandering Call

I stand at the threshold, the wind in my face,
A servant awaiting his God-appointed place.
Yet here in my village, my voice is stilled,
A prophet unwelcomed, his purpose unfulfilled.

From Freetown's shores to Zimbabwe's plains,
Eldoret whispers, Bukoba remains.
Kampala echoes with Alexandrian pride,
While Moscow beckons, a world stretched wide.

◇ (Chorus)
Oh, the path is long, the way unclear,
Yet I wait in faith, though burdened with fear.
Across the seas, the Spirit moves free,
When will it come to rest in me? ◇

New York dreams, Boston stirs,
Shanghai listens as Moscow confers.
Patriarchs gather, their voices blend,
Yet the bonds of tradition refuse to bend.
The canons speak, yet the Spirit yearns,
For a world united, where no one spurns.
Bishops, presbyters, crossing the tide,
To heal the wounded, to stand beside.

◇ **(Chorus)**
Oh, the path is long, the way unclear,
Yet I wait in faith, though burdened with fear.
Across the seas, the Spirit moves free,
When will it come to rest in me? ◇

What are the walls that keep us apart?
Are they written in stone or carved in the heart?
For the call of Christ knows no divide,
No city, no nation, no earthly pride.

In Freetown's love, a warm embrace,
Eldoret stands with a guarded face.
Zimbabwe sings of fields so vast,
While Kampala clings to the ancient past.

◇ **(Bridge)**
O Spirit, who breathes where You will,
Break these chains, teach us still.
That we are one, though paths diverge,
In Your great love, let nations converge. ◇

Bukoba waits, her arms outstretched,
While my hands remain, by duty, wretched.
Pictures I take, a silent plea,
When will the blessing be granted to me?

Yet patience blooms where doubt would tread,
A flower of hope where tears are shed.
For in this waiting, my heart grows strong,
Knowing God's plan is never wrong.

◇ (**Final Chorus**)
Oh, the path is long, the way unclear,
Yet I wait in faith, though burdened with fear.
Across the seas, the Spirit moves free,
When will it come to rest in me? ◇

So let the Fathers speak and the Prelates roam,
Across the world, building one home.
For the Church is vast, its mission one,
To serve all nations under the Son.

◇ (**Outro**)
May the walls crumble, may the borders fall,
For Christ's great Church must answer the call.
In unity's light, may we all see,
The Spirit's work in you and me. ◇

Silent Cross

Beneath the robes, beneath the light,
A struggle brews, hidden from sight.
The priest who stands to serve and give,
Carries a weight no soul can outlive.

By his side, a partner's role,
Her silent strength, her burdened soul.
Yet whispers rise from the pews below,
Of trials unseen, of seeds that sow.

◈ **(Chorus)**
Oh, the road is narrow, the burden steep,
A vow once made, a promise to keep.
But where is the peace, the joy, the rest,
When hearts are torn in love's own test? ◈

For she, the Presbytera, the unseen light,
Toils in the shadows, fights silent fights.
A wife, a mother, a caretaker true,
Her hands bear more than her share of the pew.
Yet sometimes the weight is too much to bear,
A calling shared becomes despair.
Did we ask too little? Did we ask too much?
Of the sacred union, of their human touch?

◈ **(Chorus)**
Oh, the road is narrow, the burden steep,
A vow once made, a promise to keep.
But where is the peace, the joy, the rest,
When hearts are torn in love's own test? ◈

Is it Eve's curse, the ancient fall,
Or the Church's structure, standing tall?
Is it human nature, the marriage strain,
Or the price of love in service's name?

A priest who falters without his bride,
Is like a boat adrift in the tide.
Yet to force a union, unripe, untrue,
Is to place the cross on shoulders two.

◈ **(Bridge)**
O Lord, who sees the hidden pain,
Guide their steps, make clear the lane.
For in this bond, Your will must rest,
With wisdom's care, their hearts be blessed. ◈

To choose, to wait, to teach, to know,
Before the seed of calling can grow.
For forced unions bring only strife,
A Golgotha pain to husband and wife.

Let not the faithful carry the blame,
For trials of life, for guilt or shame.
The wicked prosper, the righteous bend,
Yet God's justice reigns at the journey's end.

◇ (**Chorus**)
Oh, the road is narrow, the burden steep,
A vow once made, a promise to keep.
But where is the peace, the joy, the rest,
When hearts are torn in love's own test? ◇

So here we stand, with open hearts,
To heal the wounds, to mend the parts.
For priest and wife, a shared embrace,
A sacred calling, a holy space.

◇ (**Outro**)
May wisdom guide, may love endure,
In every trial, let faith be sure.
For the Church will thrive when hearts align,
In God's great plan, His holy design. ◇

Paths We Choose

A question came, gentle, clear,
Would you wish your sons to be like you, my dear?
I paused, uncertain, the answer unclear,
Yet wisdom whispered, "Yes, without fear."

Let them walk where their hearts will lead,
With roots in faith, their spirits freed.
Not to stray from the Orthodox way,
But to carve their journey, come what may.

◇ **(Chorus)**
Oh, the path we choose, the steps we take,
In faith and love, no hearts shall break.
For here, for there, wherever we roam,
We build our family, our earthly home. ◇

Another asked, "Would you stay awhile,
To work for gold, to stack your pile?"
I smiled and said, "No, I must be,
A guide to my people, by their side, free."

For treasures here are fleeting at best,
But service eternal brings peaceful rest.
He nodded, wise, "Your path is true,

70

For what is promised, you must pursue."

◈ (Chorus)
Oh, the path we choose, the steps we take,
In faith and love, no hearts shall break.
For here, for there, wherever we roam,
We build our family, our earthly home. ◈

"Do you miss your home, your kin, your place?"
He asked with wonder, studying my face.
I said, "No, for all are mine,
Every soul, in every clime."

Home is where my heart resides,
In distant lands or by riversides.
And he replied, "You think as we,
Living home away from home, free."

◈ (Bridge)
O Lord, who leads the wanderer's way,
Guide our hearts, come what may.
Teach us love in all we do,
To find our home in serving You. ◈

So what shall we do, this Fall, this Spring?
Shall we plant new seeds, let joy take wing?
Or labor hard in Summer's heat,
To build a world where all may meet?

Let us love, let us give, let us pray,
For tomorrow's light and today's way.

In every season, in every land,
We hold each other with helping hand.

◈ (Chorus)
Oh, the path we choose, the steps we take,
In faith and love, no hearts shall break.
For here, for there, wherever we roam,
We build our family, our earthly home. ◈

Be it Fall's retreat or Spring's embrace,
Or Summer's toil in a distant place,
May we walk together, hearts entwined,
A holy family, in God's design.

◈ (Outro)
For the path we choose, the life we live,
Is marked by love, the will to give.
Here, there, or anywhere we stay,
God is our home, our guiding way. ◈

Weaving of Two Threads

Beneath the stars, two threads were spun,
A sacred bond where two become one.
Joined in love, in vows divine,
A mystery woven by God's design.

But winds may rise, and tempests roar,
What once was whole may seem no more.
The cobwebs unravel, the pattern frays,
And hearts cry out in their broken ways.

◇ **(Chorus)**
Oh, the Textile of love is torn,
Yet grace remains where hearts are worn.
Through trials deep and shadows wide,
God still walks where love abides. ◇

One turns to paths of a second flame,
A fire that burns with another's name.
The children watch with eyes so wide,
What of the vow? What of the bride?

Another seeks to sever the chain,
A love betrayed, a heart in pain.
With years behind and children gone,

Where is the bond to carry on?

◇ **(Chorus)**
Oh, the Fabric of love is torn,
Yet grace remains where hearts are worn.
Through trials deep and shadows wide,
God still walks where love abides. ◇

And yet a third, in search of the new,
Leaves the faith that once was true.
Trendy, good, a fleeting way,
Yet where does God in this choice stay?

Do we forget what marriage means,
A sacred vow that redeems?
"For as I and the Father are one,"
Should not the threads remain unspun?

◇ **(Bridge)**
O Lord, who sees the deepest pain,
Teach us patience, help us sustain.
For in Hosea's love, we find the call,
To love, forgive, and endure it all. ◇

Where is the place for breaking apart?
For divorce that severs heart from heart?
Yet where is the place for patience true,
To bind the wounds and make all new?

The answer lies in grace divine,
A love unending, a sacred sign.

To seek God's will, to humbly pray,
And trust His light to guide our way.

◈ (**Final Chorus**)
Oh, the Fabric of love is torn,
Yet grace remains where hearts are worn.
Through trials deep and shadows wide,
God still walks where love abides. ◈

For marriage is more than words or ties,
It's a journey where true love never dies.
Through pain, through loss, through joy untold,
The threads of faith are stitched with gold.

◈ (**Outro**)
So may the broken find their way,
Through patience, love, and God's sway.
For in the weaving of life's threads true,
His mercy makes all things new. ◈

Threads of the Human Text

We are the weavers, fragile, flawed,
Binding our lives with threads from God.
Each knot a story, each line a choice,
Each thread a whisper of heart's own voice.

A brother seeks what seems amiss,
Another love, another kiss.
A vow once made, now torn in two,
Yet love still calls, "What will you do?"

The mother leaves, her gaze elsewhere,
A career that shines, a burden to bear.
Children distant, a father alone,
Where is the bond that was once our own?

A soul departs, its faith grown cold,
Drawn to what seems fresh, yet old.
"Trendy and good," the world proclaims,
Yet whispers echo of sacred names.

We falter, we stumble, we break and fall,
Yet grace still waits to answer the call.
Not in anger, not in blame,
But in the stillness, love remains.

Marriage is a mystery, a holy space,
A union bound by infinite grace.
Not just two, but the sacred three,
A mirror of God's own unity.

Where is the room for pain, for loss?
For burdens heavy, for love's great cost?
Is it in leaving, or staying true?
The answer lies in what we do.

To forgive, as Hosea once forgave,
To call back love from the silent grave.
To endure when patience wears so thin,
To find God's strength where ours has been.

Yet there is space for release, for peace,
For setting free so hearts may cease
To wage the war of love's despair,
For God still walks with us, even there.

So let us weave with gentler hands,
To understand, to meet demands.
Not with judgment, not with scorn,
But with the grace that hearts adorn.

The threads are frayed, the colors clash,
Yet in God's loom, they blend and flash.
A Textile of trials and tears,
Woven through the fleeting years.

For the brother, the mother, the wandering soul,
Each seeks the place where they'll be whole.
And in their paths, though far they stray,
God still calls, "Come this way."

To the husband whose wife is gone,
To the father waiting for the dawn,
To the faithful, the faltered, the weary, the wise,
God's mercy shines where love never dies.
Let us not curse what we cannot mend,
Nor forget that love does not easily end.
In every thread, in every seam,
Lies the hope of a greater dream.

We are the weavers, fragile, flawed,
Binding our lives with threads from God.
Each knot a story, each tear a plea,
Each stitch a step toward eternity.

Matron of Many Paths

She came, a stranger to their home,
With quiet strength, her heart alone.
The walls were cold, the stares were steel,
Yet she embraced what she could not heal.

A love unspoken, a choice so rare,
To walk a road of burdens bare.
A mother to children not her own,
Her kindness planted where hate had grown.

◇ (Chorus)
Oh, the heart that loves despite the thorn,
A beacon of grace through night and morn.
She bore the weight, she paid the cost,
For love redeemed what seemed so lost. ◇

In time, her arms would cradle life,
Eleven born from love, not strife.
Yet shadows lingered, whispers burned,
A mother's love was not returned.
The firstborn's eyes refused to see,
The gift she brought so selflessly.
The second, the third, with hardened hands,
Built walls no love could yet withstand.

◇ **(Chorus)**
Oh, the heart that loves despite the thorn,
A beacon of grace through night and morn.
She bore the weight, she paid the cost,
For love redeemed what seemed so lost. ◇

Her husband, too, a servant kind,
Was martyred by those he'd left behind.
She bore the grief, the bitter sting,
And yet found peace in the songs she'd sing.

A widow now, her days grow long,
Yet still she hums a patient song.
For even the kicks of ingrate kin,
Cannot erase the love within.

◇ **(Bridge)**
O Lord, who sees the hidden strife,
Bless the heart that gives its life.
For every thorn and every tear,
Your mercy's hand will hold her near. ◇

Her story mirrors many untold,
Of love unyielding, brave and bold.
For she became both rock and tree,
Sheltering those who could not see.

The children she bore, the children she raised,
Each carry marks of paths she paved.
And though the scars may never fade,
Her legacy will not be swayed.

◇ (**Final Chorus**)
Oh, the heart that loves despite the thorn,
A beacon of grace through night and morn.
She bore the weight, she paid the cost,
For love redeemed what seemed so lost. ◇

Now as the years turn skies to gray,
Her spirit shines like break of day.
A matron of paths, of wounds, of care,
A love eternal, beyond compare.

◇ (**Outro**)
Let her story ring, let her courage flow,
For all who love where others won't go.
In her life, a truth divine,
A glimpse of God's own love in time. ◇

The Unseen Pillar

He began as a servant in a quiet abode,
Where faith took root and love bestowed.
A houseboy, unseen, yet keen to learn,
The fires of wisdom within him burned.

Years passed, and he rose with grace,
A trusted hand in a sacred place.
From humble halls to hallowed ground,
A spirit steadfast, his purpose found.

◈ **(Chorus)**
Oh, the unseen pillar, steady and strong,
A guiding hand where hearts belong.
He gave his all, though none could see,
The quiet force of humility. ◈

An educator's path he chose to tread,
To shape young minds, to forge ahead.
In schools of faith where welcome was rare,
He worked with love, beyond despair.

Proclaimed the best in a golden year,
He stood on heights both bright and clear.
From the lowliest schools, he raised the name,

And left them shining, no more the same.

◇ **(Chorus)**
Oh, the unseen pillar, steady and strong,
A guiding hand where hearts belong.
He gave his all, though none could see,
The quiet force of humility. ◇

A headmaster, a builder of dreams,
A man of purpose, not idle schemes.
Yet in his village, the heart would ache,
For love unreturned, for joy at stake.

His children chose to give, not take,
To help the village, for others' sake.
And though their hearts were pure and true,
He longed for honor they never knew.

◇ **(Bridge)**
O Lord, who sees the silent pain,
Bless the hearts that give in vain.
For every act, though unadmired,
Is in Your book, forever inspired. ◇

When his life was taken by hands he taught,
The irony deep, the lessons fraught.
Yet his legacy lives in the seeds he sown,
In the countless hearts his love had grown.

A father, a mentor, a steadfast guide,
With resilience firm, with faith as his bride.

From Sarah's care and Ibrahim's name,
He rose to greatness, beyond acclaim.

◈ (**Final Chorus**)
Oh, the unseen pillar, steady and strong,
A guiding hand where hearts belong.
He gave his all, though none could see,
The quiet force of humility. ◈

Now he rests, his work complete,
In heaven's arms, at the Savior's feet.
And though the world may not have known,
His deeds are etched in God's own throne.

◈ (**Outro**)
Let his story ring, let his life inspire,
A beacon of hope, a holy fire.
For in his journey, we see the light,
Of a soul who lived for what was right. ◈

The Spectacles Found

There was a man, his gaze now bare,
Who searched for his sight with a wandering stare.
His spectacles gone, misplaced, unseen,
A riddle of vision where none had been.

He checked his pockets, the table, the chair,
Touched his face with a growing despair.
His sockets were empty, his hope grew thin,
For the world around was blurring within.

◈ **(Chorus)**
Oh, the eyes that strain, the hands that seek,
In the quiet of loss, the vision is weak.
Yet through the blur, the path will show,
For what is misplaced, we'll surely know. ◈

Two others passed, with their glasses in hand,
And a third who gazed with eyes unplanned.
They saw the frames, so simple, so worn,
And knew they belonged where sight was torn.
The first, with specs, turned the find to light,
"This is his vision, his borrowed sight."
The second agreed, with a nod sincere,
"For without them, his world is unclear."

◇ (**Chorus**)
Oh, the eyes that strain, the hands that seek,
In the quiet of loss, the vision is weak.
Yet through the blur, the path will show,
For what is misplaced, we'll surely know. ◇

The third, with bare eyes, no specs to wear,
Carried the treasure with tender care.
To the man who searched, they brought the gift,
Restoring the world in a moment swift.

He placed them gently upon his face,
And the lines of life returned to place.
With grateful heart and a humbled soul,
He saw the kindness that made him whole.

◇ (**Bridge**)
O the gift of sight, not just through the lens,
But the hands of strangers, the love of friends.
For vision is more than what eyes can see,
It's the grace of others that sets us free. ◇

And so the man, with his specs restored,
Saw not just the world, but the gift they poured.
For those who see with hearts so clear,
Bring light to the blind and draw them near.

◇ (**Final Chorus**)
Oh, the eyes that strain, the hands that seek,
In the quiet of loss, the vision is weak.
Yet through the blur, the path will show,

For what is misplaced, we'll surely know. ◈

So, let us be like the two who see,
And the third who carried, so humbly.
For in the giving, the finding, the care,
We bring light to darkness, a gift to share.

Allegory of Two the Mothers

(Based on Galatians 4:22-27)

In days of old, two mothers stood,
Their paths entwined as life deemed good.
One bore a child in chains and toil,
The other's son through promise royal.

The first, a servant bound by fate,
Her child born to a life innate.
Her name was Hagar, her station low,
From Mount Sinai, her children flow.

She bore the weight of Sinai's call,
A covenant etched for one and all.
But slavery binds where freedom wanes,
A legacy marked by earthly chains.

The second, free, her name unknown,
Her child a seed of grace alone.
Not by flesh, but by a word,
A promise kept, her spirit stirred.

She is the mother of heights above,
Jerusalem's womb of eternal love.

Not bound by earth, her children sing,
A chorus of joy to their heavenly King.

◈ **(Chorus)**
Rejoice, O barren, break forth and cry,
For children abound where hope draws nigh.
From desolation springs life anew,
A mother of freedom, her promise true. ◈

Two mothers, two covenants, two ways to live,
One bound by law, the other to give.
For flesh may toil, but promise flies,
Beyond the earth to the open skies.

So, brethren, hear this sacred tale,
Of grace that triumphs where flesh must fail.
For the Jerusalem above is our home,
A city of light where we shall roam.

◈ **(Final Chorus)**
Rejoice, O barren, break forth and cry,
For children abound where hope draws nigh.
From desolation springs life anew,
A mother of freedom, her promise true. ◈

Light on the Stand

(Based on Luke 8:16-21)

No lamp is lit to hide away,
Its purpose lost in shadow's sway.
But raised on high, its glow is shown,
A beacon bright, a truth made known.

The light of Christ, a flame divine,
To guide the lost, to clearly shine.
No secret veiled, no truth concealed,
For in His light, all is revealed.

◈ **(Chorus)**
Let the lamp stand tall, let the flame burn bright,
To scatter the dark, to banish the night.
For all shall be seen, all hidden made clear,
In the light of His truth, no shadows appear. ◈

Take heed, O soul, in what you hear,
For wisdom grows when hearts draw near.
To those who have, abundance flows,
But from the hollow, all shall close.

For a heart that hoards, yet never gives,

Loses the light by which it lives.
But one who shares, who loves, who learns,
Kindles the fire that ever burns.

◇ **(Chorus)**
Let the lamp stand tall, let the flame burn bright,
To scatter the dark, to banish the night.
For all shall be seen, all hidden made clear,
In the light of His truth, no shadows appear. ◇

Then came His family, seeking their place,
But the Lord spoke words of boundless grace:
"My mother, my brothers are those who hear,
The word of God, and hold it near."

Not bound by blood, but by love's decree,
The family of God is wide and free.
For those who hear and those who do,
Are the kin of Christ, both old and new.

◇ **(Final Chorus)**
Let the lamp stand tall, let the flame burn bright,
To scatter the dark, to banish the night.
For all shall be seen, all hidden made clear,
In the light of His truth, no shadows appear. ◇

So light your lamp, and let it show,
The path of love, the way to go.
For in His light, we walk, we stand,
A family united, hand in hand.

Voices in the Forest

Visit me, talk to me, stay for a while,
In the heart of this forest, where shadows beguile.
Tell them for me, what the leaves cannot say,
Stand by me, guide me through the fray.

Deep in the forest, where whispers rise,
Hope and despair wear their shared disguise.
The trees have seen what we cannot know,
Their roots hold stories of long ago.

◇ (Chorus)
Oh, voices that call from the forest deep,
Where secrets linger and spirits weep.
Hope and despair, entwined they sing,
Of days gone by and what love can bring. ◇

A voice of hope speaks soft but clear,
"I'm here with you, cast off your fear."
It dances with light through the canopy high,
A thread of gold in the shadowed sky.

But despair replies, in a mournful tone,
"I've walked these paths, I am not alone."
It clings to the damp, to the earth below,

A shadow that follows wherever we go.

◈ (**Chorus**)
Oh, voices that call from the forest deep,
Where secrets linger and spirits weep.
Hope and despair, entwined they sing,
Of days gone by and what love can bring. ◈

The trees stand silent, yet they know well,
The tales of triumph, the times we fell.
The cries of battles, the songs of peace,
The longing for life, the final release.

Visit me, where the rivers run,
Where the forest bathes in the morning sun.
Talk to me, where the echoes play,
Where night meets dawn, and dark meets day.

◈ (**Bridge**)
O forest of wisdom, hold us tight,
Teach us to see through shadow and light.
For hope may falter, but it won't depart,
And despair is softened by a steadfast heart. ◈

So let the voices weave their tale,
Through ancient roots and trails frail.
Tell them for me, the ones who wait,
That love can conquer even fate.

Stand by me, where the stories flow,
Through the whispers of trees, where mysteries grow.

For hope and despair are two of a kind,
Both leading us to the truths we find.

◈ (**Final Chorus**)
Oh, voices that call from the forest deep,
Where secrets linger and spirits weep.
Hope and despair, entwined they sing,
Of days gone by and what love can bring. ◈

Visit me, talk to me, stay for a while,
In the heart of this forest, where shadows beguile.
Stand by me, in this sacred place,
Where hope takes root and despair finds grace.

The Journey Ahead

My dear son, I hear your voice,
The weight of change, the fear of choice.
To leave the known, the path you know,
For fields where brighter chances grow.

You see the road as long and steep,
A mountain high, a climb so deep.
Yet sometimes change, though hard to bear,
Can open skies beyond compare.

◇ (Chorus)
Oh, the world is wide, the path is new,
With challenges waiting to strengthen you.
A leap of faith, a step to start,
To find your way and grow your heart. ◇

The school you leave has taught you much,
Its lessons linger, its gentle touch.
But there are worlds beyond these walls,
Where greater dreams and purpose calls.

In Uganda's soil, your roots run deep,
But the skies of the world await your leap.
The USA, a field untamed,

A place where goals are boldly claimed.

◇ (Chorus)
Oh, the world is wide, the path is new,
With challenges waiting to strengthen you.
A leap of faith, a step to start,
To find your way and grow your heart. ◇

I know you fear the time it takes,
The unfamiliar paths it makes.
But time's a teacher, patient and kind,
Revealing treasures for those who find.

Think not of years, but of the gain,
The skills, the knowledge, the strength through pain.
Each challenge faced, each trial endured,
A future brighter, a path assured.

◇ (Bridge)
Oh, my son, the world is vast,
The moments fleeting, the time moves fast.
But courage leads where fear may bind,
And greater truths you'll surely find. ◇

You learn in ways unique, your own,
A mind where seeds of brilliance are sown.
In every move, in every stride,
A chance to grow, to turn the tide.

So take this step, though hard it seems,
To chase your hopes, to build your dreams.

The world's your canvas, vast and wide,
And I'll be with you, by your side.

◈ (**Final Chorus**)
Oh, the world is wide, the path is new,
With challenges waiting to strengthen you.
A leap of faith, a step to start,
To find your way and grow your heart. ◈

My son, remember, wherever you go,
Your roots in Uganda will always show.
But wings must spread for dreams to soar,
And the world is waiting beyond the door.

Take courage, my child, embrace the call,
For in every journey, you'll grow tall.
The USA beckons, with lessons and light,
A place to sharpen your gifted sight.

◈ (**Outro**)
So step with hope, let your fears fade,
The world is yours, be not afraid.
For in every step, in every mile,
You'll find your strength and wear your smile. ◈

The Greek Wall

(Inspired by my Koine Greek Teacher, 12/ 09/2024)

"Hit your head upon the Greek wall,
And watch as letters begin to fall."
From Alpha to Omega, their stories unfold,
A language ancient, a treasure of gold.

First, learn the letters, the sacred key,
To unlock the words of eternity.
Alpha and Beta, Gamma, too,
Delta's curve and Epsilon's hue.

◈ **(Chorus)**
Oh, Greek of old, your wisdom calls,
Through ancient words, your beauty enthralls.
I'll walk this path, I'll learn, I'll strive,
To make your truth come alive. ◈

Next comes the case, the nouns to bend,
From subject to object, their forms extend.
Nominative shines as the sentence head,
Genitive whispers of what's been said.

Dative gives, Accusative takes,

Vocative calls with the sound it makes.
Each case a thread in the grammar's weave,
A pattern of meaning we must perceive.

◈ (**Chorus**)
Oh, Greek of old, your wisdom calls,
Through ancient words, your beauty enthralls.
I'll walk this path, I'll learn, I'll strive,
To make your truth come alive. ◈

Now to the verbs, the heart of the tale,
With tense and voice, they never fail.
Present speaks of what's here and now,
Imperfect recalls the when and how.

Aorist strikes with a timeless flair,
Perfect completes what lingers there.
Future's promise, a path untried,
Middle and Passive, action's guide.

◈ (**Bridge**)
O Lord, who spoke in this tongue so fine,
Help me to master its sacred design.
For every paradigm, each word I learn,
Brings me closer to Your truth to discern. ◈

Adjectives, adverbs, their forms abound,
With layers of meaning, their depth profound.
Prepositions dance, a guiding thread,
Through phrases crafted, by Spirit led.

Syntax and structure, a challenge to meet,
Each clause a step in this walk complete.
For Greek is a journey, a mountain to climb,
A labor of love through rhythm and rhyme.

◈ (Chorus)
Oh, Greek of old, your wisdom calls,
Through ancient words, your beauty enthralls.
I'll walk this path, I'll learn, I'll strive,
To make your truth come alive. ◈

So hit your head upon the Greek wall,
And know with each strike, you're learning it all.
For every stumble, each step you take,
Brings you closer to the truth you'll make.

Augment the verbs, the stems align,
Master the paradigms, one at a time.
Declensions three, their endings clear,
With every effort, the Word draws near.

◈ (Final Chorus)
Oh, Greek of old, your wisdom calls,
Through ancient words, your beauty enthralls.
I'll walk this path, I'll learn, I'll strive,
To make your truth come alive. ◈

In time, the wall will crumble away,
And Greek will sing with the words you say.
For the language of Scripture, pure and true,
Is a gift of grace, waiting for you.

The Word to Loosen: Λύω

Let us loosen, let us untie,
The meaning of λύω as we strive and apply.
A word so simple, yet vast in its reach,
In every form, there's a lesson to teach.

In its **Present Active**, λύω stands,
"I loosen," it says, with firm command.
Continuous action, unfolding in time,
The present tense, so rhythmic, sublime.

◈ (**Chorus**)
Oh, λύω, to loosen, to free, to unbind,
A word of release, both gentle and kind.
In every form, your meaning is clear,
To unlock the truth, to draw us near. ◈

In **Future Active**, λύσω shines,
"I will loosen," across the lines.
A promise spoken, an act to come,
Anticipation beats like a drum.

The **Aorist Active**, ἔλυσα proclaims,
"I loosened," it states, unbound by chains.
A moment past, a deed complete,

In timeless grace, its work replete.

◈ (**Chorus**)
Oh, λύω, to loosen, to free, to unbind,
A word of release, both gentle and kind.
In every form, your meaning is clear,
To unlock the truth, to draw us near. ◈

In the **Perfect Active**, λέλυκα reigns,
"I have loosened," the act remains.
A finished work, yet effects endure,
In this form, the meaning is sure.

Then comes the **Passive**, λύομαι to say,
"I am being loosened," in this display.
The subject receives, the action is done,
A quiet release by another begun.

◈ (**Bridge**)
Oh, λύω, a key to unlock the chains,
In voice and tense, your meaning remains.
From present to perfect, from passive to strong,
Your forms create a liberating song. ◈

In **Middle Voice**, λύομαι sings,
"I loosen for myself," the freedom it brings.
An act reflective, a choice refined,
To loose one's soul, to ease one's mind.

From **Imperative**—λύε, "loosen now!"
To **Subjunctive**—λύωμεν, "may we loosen, somehow."

The moods and modes, they shift and play,
In each, the meaning finds its way.

◇ (Final Chorus)

Oh, λύω, to loosen, to free, to unbind,
A word of release, both gentle and kind.
In every form, your meaning is clear,
To unlock the truth, to draw us near. ◇

So loosen the chains, unbind the heart,
Through λύω, the journey can start.
In every tense, in every voice,
The word to loosen gives us a choice.

To loosen is more than a word to recite,
It carries a freedom, a guiding light.
For in the grammar of λύω, we see,
A path to explore, a key to be free.

In **Infinitive**, λύειν softly declares,
"To loosen," a purpose that always prepares.
Timeless and neutral, it calmly unfolds,
The essence of action, a truth it holds.

The **Participle**, λύων, stands apart,
"Loosening," it says, with a present heart.
Continuous motion, an act in progress,
Unbinding the soul from fear's regress.

◇ (Chorus)

Oh, λύω, to loosen, to free, to unbind,

A word of release, both gentle and kind.
In every form, your meaning is clear,
To unlock the truth, to draw us near. ◈

And then the Passive, rich with grace,
Λυθείς, "having been loosened," takes its place.
A deed completed, a freedom bestowed,
By the hand of another, the burden unloads.

In **Optative**, λυοίμην dreams,
"May I loosen," it quietly gleams.
A wish, a hope, in this subtle tone,
For chains to break and truth be shown.

◈ **(Bridge)**
Oh, λύω, a mirror to what we seek,
In every form, its voice will speak.
Through tense and mood, through heart and mind,
A timeless lesson in freedom we find. ◈

So learn the forms, each voice, each tense,
Each paradigm a new defense.
For λύω is more than grammar's tool,
It teaches the way of love's golden rule.

To loosen anger, to unbind fear,
To break the chains that keep others near.
In the language of Greek, a message profound,
In every form, grace is found.

◈ **(Final Chorus)**

Oh, λύω, to loosen, to free, to unbind,
A word of release, both gentle and kind.
In every form, your meaning is clear,
To unlock the truth, to draw us near. ◇

So hit your head on the Greek wall once more,
Let λύω's wisdom your spirit restore.
For in its forms, a journey awaits,
To loosen the soul and open the gates.

Through λύω's lens, the Scriptures unfold,
Stories of freedom, both ancient and bold.
Christ's own words, in Greek they came,
To loosen our burdens, to heal our shame.

"Loose him and let him go," they cried,
When Lazarus rose, no longer tied.
The bonds of death, the grave's tight hold,
Loosened by grace, as the prophets told.

In parables taught and miracles wrought,
The power of λύω was clearly sought.
To unbind the sinner, to free the slave,
To loosen the grip of the cold, dark grave.

◇ (Chorus)
Oh, λύω, to loosen, to free, to unbind,
A word of salvation for all mankind.
In the Scriptures clear, your truth we see,
To loosen the soul and set it free. ◇

Through λύω's forms, we hear the call,
To break the chains that bind us all.
In the Present tense, we act today,
In the Future, hope lights the way.

The Aorist reminds of what has been done,
A single act where freedom's won.
In Perfect tense, the work complete,
The gift of grace is made replete.

◇ (Bridge)
Oh, λύω, in you we find,
A lesson of love for all mankind.
To loosen, to heal, to lift, to restore,
A call to unbind forevermore. ◇

To master λύω is more than the tongue,
It's a journey begun where life is sung.
Each form a step, each tense a guide,
To walk the path where love abides.

So take the task, though the road is long,
And let λύω's wisdom make you strong.
For in the study of words so deep,
The mysteries of freedom you will reap.

◇ (Final Chorus)
Oh, λύω, to loosen, to free, to unbind,
A word of salvation for all mankind.
In the Scriptures clear, your truth we see,
To loosen the soul and set it free. ◇

Through λύω's grace, the walls will fall,
Its power of freedom will conquer all.
So learn, endure, and let it be known,
That λύω's truth leads us home.

The Aorist Forms of Λύω

In the Aorist tense, we take our stand,
A moment of action, a deed so grand.
ἔλυσα speaks, "I have loosened, it's done,"
A single act where freedom is won.

The story is brief, the action complete,
A snapshot of time, a work replete.
No lingering threads, no endless play,
The Aorist moves in a timeless way.

◇ (Chorus)
Oh, Aorist tense, a flash in time,
A single act, a perfect climb.
Through λύω's forms, your voice is clear,
The power to free is ever near. ◇

To the Middle Voice, we turn our ear,
ἐλυσαμην, "I have loosened for myself," we hear.
A deed reflective, an inward grace,
To unbind the heart in its sacred space.

Then comes the Passive, soft yet profound,
ἐλύθην, "I was loosened," the chains unbound.
Not by my hand, but by one unseen,
A gift of freedom, a life redeemed.

◇ (Chorus)
Oh, Aorist tense, a flash in time,
A single act, a perfect climb.
Through λύω's forms, your voice is clear,
The power to free is ever near. ◇

In the Aorist Subjunctive, λύσω we pray,
"May I loosen," to guide the way.
A hope for freedom, a choice untold,
A future unbound, a story bold.

The Optative follows, λύσαιμι's plea,
"Would that I loosen," a wish set free.
A softer tone, a yearning deep,
For chains to break, for peace to keep.

◇ (Bridge)
Oh, Aorist forms, you speak so true,
A moment of action, a timeless view.
From voice to mood, your wisdom flows,
A path of freedom, where life bestows. ◇

The Imperative speaks, λῦσον commands,
"Loosen now!" with determined hands.
To act, to free, to take the stand,
To break the chains at love's demand.

The Infinitive follows, λῦσαι serene,
"To loosen," it whispers, with purpose keen.
Not bound by time, a state of mind,
A timeless call to free mankind.

◇ (Final Chorus)
Oh, Aorist tense, a flash in time,
A single act, a perfect climb.
Through λύω's forms, your voice is clear,
The power to free is ever near. ◇

In every form, in every phrase,
The Aorist shines through ancient days.
A moment's act, a freedom won,

Through λύω's truth, our work is done.

So take the Aorist, let it be known,
Its power to loosen has always shown.
A timeless gift, a freedom call,
Through λύω's forms, we conquer all.

Depth of Aorist Forms

In λύω's Aorist, the stories unfold,
Moments of action, both daring and bold.
The past is captured, yet timeless it stays,
Binding the fleeting to eternal ways.

Active Indicative, ἔλυσα begins,
"I loosened," it tells of where freedom begins.
The chains are broken, the deed is complete,
A decisive act, a grace so sweet.

Then **Middle Indicative**, ἐλυσάμην we say,
"I loosened for myself," to clear the way.
Not selfish, but careful, to tend the soul,
To unbind the heart, to make it whole.

◇ **(Chorus)**
Oh, Aorist forms, your wisdom shines,
Through moments of action, across all times.
You teach us to act, to loosen, to free,
The timeless gift of eternity. ◇

In the **Passive Indicative**, ἐλύθην we find,
"I was loosened," by a force more kind.
Not by my power, but mercy untold,

My chains fell away, my spirit consoled.

The **Subjunctive Active**, λύσω, appears,
"May I loosen," it whispers through fears.
A prayer for freedom, a call to the skies,
To act with courage, to open blind eyes.

The **Subjunctive Passive**, λυθῶ, we sing,
"May I be loosened," by heaven's King.
A plea for release, from bondage and pain,
To be freed by grace, to live again.

◇ (**Chorus**)
Oh, Aorist forms, your wisdom shines,
Through moments of action, across all times.
You teach us to act, to loosen, to free,
The timeless gift of eternity. ◇

The **Imperative Active**, λύσον commands,
"Loosen now!" with purposeful hands.
A call to break what binds us tight,
To step into freedom, to claim the light.

The **Imperative Passive**, λυθῆτι pleads,
"Be loosened," it asks for the soul's needs.
An invitation to let go, to receive,
The freedom that faith compels us to believe.

◇ (**Bridge**)
Oh, λύω's forms, so rich, so vast,
A treasure of meaning from the ancient past.

Through Active, Middle, and Passive, you show,
The depths of freedom we come to know. ◈

The **Infinitive Active**, λύσαι serene,
"To loosen," it whispers, with a voice unseen.
It captures the essence, beyond all time,
An eternal call, a rhythm, a rhyme.

The **Infinitive Passive**, λυθῆναι proclaims,
"To be loosened," by mercy's flames.
A quiet surrender, a trust so deep,
In the arms of grace, our spirits leap.

◈ (**Final Chorus**)
Oh, Aorist forms, your wisdom shines,
Through moments of action, across all times.
You teach us to act, to loosen, to free,
The timeless gift of eternity. ◈

So walk with λύω, let Aorist lead,
Through forms and meanings, through thought and deed.
For in every tense, in every voice,
The power to loosen is a divine choice.

Embrace the Aorist, the moments it shows,
Through each sacred form, your knowledge grows.
In loosening bonds, in setting free,
You master the gift of eternity.

War in the Middle East

A storm brews beneath the ancient skies,
Where prophets once walked, where truth now dies.
The land of promise, now soaked in despair,
Each breath a prayer, each silence a snare.

Israel burns with wounds untold,
Syria bleeds where hearts grow cold.
Lebanon cries through shattered streets,
A harmony fractured, a song that retreats.

◇ **(Chorus)**
Oh, land of faith, oh, cradle of light,
How have you fallen to endless night?
From the scrolls of peace to the cries of pain,
The soil is soaked with tears like rain. ◇

The neighbors watch with eyes of flame,
No victor emerges, no glory, no name.
The borders blur with bloodied hands,
A map of grief on the shifting sands.

Missiles rise where olives grew,
Tearing the earth, both old and new.
Children scream, their laughter gone,

A war without reason, marching on.

◇ (Chorus)
Oh, land of faith, oh, cradle of light,
How have you fallen to endless night?
From the scrolls of peace to the cries of pain,
The soil is soaked with tears like rain. ◇

Mountains weep, rivers run red,
Over ruins of cities, the spirits of the dead.
The cedars of Lebanon bow their heads low,
As nations crumble where hope used to grow.

Syria's plains echo with fear,
While Israel wrestles with pain severe.
Neighbors in name, yet strangers in heart,
Each wound inflicted tears worlds apart.

◇ (Bridge)
O land where prophets spoke of peace,
When will this agony find release?
The scrolls were written, the paths were drawn,
But shadows linger where light has gone. ◇

The cries ascend to the heavens above,
Where is the justice, where is the love?
The graves grow full, the fields run dry,
As innocent souls are left to die.

The war has no winner, no end in sight,
Only darkness that deepens the plight.

Yet deep in the ruins, a whisper remains,
A call for mercy amidst the chains.

◈ **(Final Chorus)**
Oh, land of faith, oh, cradle of light,
How have you fallen to endless night?
Yet in the ashes, a seed may grow,
Of peace and hope this land will know. ◈

So let the guns falter, let swords be stilled,
Let hearts be softened, and trust be rebuilt.
For the Middle East, a land of old,
Deserves a story of peace retold.

Until that day, we weep, we pray,
For the dawn to break through this endless gray.
For neighbors to hold, not harm, each other,
And see in each face a sister, a brother.

City on a Hill

You are the city, the city on a hill,
A beacon of light where the night is still.
Your towers rise, your streets proclaim,
A truth eternal, a holy name.

In the darkened world, your glow remains,
A light that cuts through the shadowed plains.
Not hidden, not veiled, not torn apart,
But shining boldly from the heart.

◈ (Chorus)
Oh, city on a hill, your light must shine,
A beacon of hope, a love divine.
Through trials deep and shadows wide,
Your light will lead, your faith will guide. ◈

Your walls are built on justice strong,
Your gates sing mercy's ancient song.
Not by power, nor by might,
But by the Spirit that gives you light.

Yet cities below, in the valley's grasp,
Have traded their honor for fleeting clasp.
The brilliance fades, the shadows grow,

A hollowed form, a pride laid low.

◈ **(Chorus)**
Oh, city on a hill, your light must shine,
A beacon of hope, a love divine.
Through trials deep and shadows wide,
Your light will lead, your faith will guide. ◈

The city above, where truth resides,
Knows service humbles, yet never hides.
Its streets are paved with the deeds of grace,
Its crown is worn with the meekest face.

For influence grows not from power's throne,
But from hearts that love, from seeds well sown.
A city that serves, that lifts the weak,
Is the city whose name all nations seek.

◈ **(Bridge)**
Oh, city on a hill, stand firm, stand bright,
Through storms and trials, keep your light.
For the world will see and hearts will turn,
To the fire of love, to the truth they yearn. ◈

Let your light so shine, let it never fade,
Through every deed, through every trade.
For the world will know by what you give,
That your city shines so others live.

Be not the city that dims its flame,
For power, for greed, for hollow name.

But rise, O hill, with faith and might,
And let the world bask in your light.

◈ (**Final Chorus**)
Oh, city on a hill, your light must shine,
A beacon of hope, a love divine.
Through trials deep and shadows wide,
Your light will lead, your faith will guide. ◈

For you are the city, the call, the way,
A light to the lost, the break of day.
And those who see will give God praise,
For the city that shines through eternal days.

Warning Flame

You are the city, the city on a hill,
With lights that shine, a call to fulfill.
Yet shadows creep, a danger grows,
A fire ignites where wisdom slows.

Drug abuse, a thief in the night,
Dims the brilliance, extinguishes light.
A city once bright, now clouded in haze,
Lost in chaos, its walls ablaze.

◇ **(Chorus)**
Oh, city on a hill, your flame must stay,
A beacon of hope to light the way.
Through smoke and ash, through trial and fight,
Take heed, rise strong, rekindle the light. ◇

The warning signs, the fire alarm rings,
A cry for rescue, a voice that sings:
"Wake up, O city, your walls are weak,
Take the instructions your Savior speaks."

The drugs deceive, they steal, they bind,
They cloud the soul, they darken the mind.
A city that falls to its own desire,

Becomes a ruin, consumed by fire.

◇ **(Chorus)**
Oh, city on a hill, your flame must stay,
A beacon of hope to light the way.
Through smoke and ash, through trial and fight,
Take heed, rise strong, rekindle the light. ◇

Listen to the call, the alarm's clear sound,
Instructions given, the way is found.
To fight the fire, to cleanse the streets,
Requires a heart that truly beats.

Stand as the city, unshaken, bold,
Turn from the shadows, break their hold.
For drugs will steal what makes you shine,
But the fire of hope is ever divine.

◇ **(Bridge)**
Oh, city on a hill, hear the alarm,
Turn from the danger, flee from harm.
Take every step to reclaim your place,
Let mercy rebuild, let love embrace. ◇

The first step is to take the hand,
Of those who guide, who understand.
Follow the plan, extinguish the blaze,
Restore the light for brighter days.

A city that learns, that heeds the call,
Will stand once more, though it may fall.

For even through smoke, the light can be,
A beacon of hope for all to see.

◈ (**Final Chorus**)
Oh, city on a hill, your flame must stay,
A beacon of hope to light the way.
Through smoke and ash, through trial and fight,
Take heed, rise strong, rekindle the light. ◈

So let your light shine, through fire and storm,
A city renewed, a life transformed.
For those who see will turn and praise,
The city that shines through eternal days.

Shelter of Hope

You are the city, the city on a hill,
A beacon of light where love fulfills.
For the sick, the homeless, the suffering souls,
Your light must shine, your heart must hold.

The seniors bent by the weight of years,
Their faces lined with countless tears.
The sick who long for healing's touch,
The homeless yearning for just so much.

◇ (**Chorus**)
Oh, city on a hill, a refuge bright,
A shelter of hope through the darkest night.
For those in pain, for those in need,
Let your love shine through every deed. ◇

The winds may howl, the storms may rage,
But you are the shelter, a holy stage.
For those who wander, for those who fall,
The city must answer the desperate call.

A warm embrace, a healing hand,
A quiet meal, a place to stand.
These simple acts, so small, so kind,

Build the city of love for all mankind.

◇ **(Chorus)**
Oh, city on a hill, a refuge bright,
A shelter of hope through the darkest night.
For those in pain, for those in need,
Let your love shine through every deed. ◇

The pensioners whisper their wisdom clear,
"Hold us close, for our end draws near."
The sick implore with voices low,
"Give us the strength to let hope grow."

The homeless wander with weary eyes,
Seeking a roof beneath the skies.
And the suffering cry, their spirits torn,
In need of a light to face the morn.

◇ **(Bridge)**
Oh, city of mercy, oh, city of grace,
Bring healing and love to every face.
Through acts of kindness, through hearts that care,
Let your light shine everywhere. ◇

For you are the city, the hands, the feet,
The place where heaven and earth will meet.
Through every soul you lift, you raise,
The world will see and give God praise.

◇ **(Final Chorus)**
Oh, city on a hill, a refuge bright,

A shelter of hope through the darkest night.
For those in pain, for those in need,
Let your love shine through every deed. ◈

So stand as the city, steadfast and strong,
A haven of hope where all belong.
For in your light, the broken will find,
A peace that restores, a love that's kind.

Keys, Doors, and Shutters

In the village kingdom where stories flow,
There are keys, doors, and shutters to show.
Each has a purpose, a role to play,
Guarding the night, welcoming the day.

The keys are small but mighty in hand,
They open the secrets of the land.
A turn, a click, a portal wide,
A passage to dreams, a place to hide.

◇ **(Chorus)**
Oh, the keys to life, the doors of grace,
In the village kingdom, each finds its place.
Through shutters closed or open wide,
The heart of the kingdom will always abide. ◇

The doors are humble, yet they hold,
Stories of new and tales of old.
Some creak with age, some stand tall,
Each one a witness to it all.

They open for strangers, for kin, for kings,
They shut against sorrow, the darkness it brings.
But a door unlocked, a welcome made,

Turns fear to friendship, night to day.

◇ **(Chorus)**
Oh, the keys to life, the doors of grace,
In the village kingdom, each finds its place.
Through shutters closed or open wide,
The heart of the kingdom will always abide. ◇

The shutters sway with the wind's command,
They shield the home, they understand.
When storms arise, they hold the line,
Protecting the light that dares to shine.

But when the sun ascends the sky,
The shutters open, and spirits fly.
A glimpse of life through the wooden frame,
A world outside, never the same.

◇ **(Bridge)**
Oh, keys unlock, and doors invite,
Shutters guard both day and night.
In the village kingdom, they stand as one,
A fortress strong, beneath the sun. ◇

For keys bring power, and doors bring choice,
Shutters conceal or let out the voice.
Each plays a part in the kingdom's tale,
Through every triumph, through every wail.

◇ **(Final Chorus)**
Oh, the keys to life, the doors of grace,

In the village kingdom, each finds its place.
Through shutters closed or open wide,
The heart of the kingdom will always abide. ◈

So cherish the keys, the doors, the shutters,
In the village kingdom where life still utters.
For in their frames, their locks, their stays,
Lies the wisdom of a thousand days.

Thornbush Rhapsody

In a field of beasts and swaying trees,
The thornbush stood with mocking ease.
"Why this one here, with robes of white,
Should seek to lead by sacred rite?"

The lion roared, "Not in our land!
We have no need of your guiding hand."
The jackal laughed, the vultures cried,
"This one must leave or be crucified."

Yet across the river, the cedar called,
"Come here, O priest, where none appalled."
The dove sang sweet, the lamb knelt low,
"Welcome, O shepherd, where peace may grow."

◇ (Chorus)
Oh, why do the thornbush rage and scorn?
Why crucify those in their homeland born?
For the cedar calls, the olive extends,
While the homeward fields forsake their friends. ◇

The priest stood silent, his roots still deep,
In soil where his fathers sowed and reap.
Yet the banyan tree, with branches wide,

129

Refused his shadow, his soul denied.

"Go to the foreign lands," they hissed,
"Take your rites where you'll be kissed.
For here the fox will tear your vine,
And mock the fruits of your sacred line."

The olive grove stretched arms of green,
"Come here, O priest, where love is seen."
The eagle soared, the streams ran free,
"Here is the place where you should be."

◈ (Chorus)
Oh, why do the thornbush rage and scorn?
Why crucify those in their homeland born?
For the cedar calls, the olive extends,
While the homeward fields forsake their friends. ◈

The hyena howled, the thornbush spread,
"This land's not yours, but ours instead."
Yet far away, the garden bloomed,
"Come here, O priest, where hearts resume."

The priest, though torn, began to tread,
Where palms arose, where roses spread.
But still he looked at the soil behind,
Where his heart was bound, his roots aligned.

◈ (Bridge)
Oh, thornbush, oh, banyan, why must you hate?
Your fruits grow bitter, your rage so great.

While cedars and olives embrace with grace,
Your land turns barren, a hollowed space. ◈

The animals feasted, the plants stood still,
The priest departed against his will.
Yet in the garden of foreign care,
He found the welcome denied him there.

And still the thornbush whispers low,
"Why should his rites here dare to grow?"
But the cedar answers, bold and free,
"Blessed is the priest who comes to me."

◈ **(Final Chorus)**
Oh, why do the thornbush rage and scorn?
Why crucify those in their homeland born?
For the cedar calls, the olive extends,
While the homeward fields forsake their friends. ◈

Let the nations rage, let the thornbush burn,
Yet truth will rise, and hearts will turn.
For the priest who walks with sacred light,
Will find his place in the world's great rite.

Tale of Shadows and Sparks

In a jungle so vast, beneath the sun's dim glow,
Where vines tangled tight and the rivers slow,
Lived beasts who toiled, their strength fading thin,
As the weight of the world bore down on their skin.

The sickness swept through like a silent breeze,
Taking the swift, the strong, the wise with ease.
Many fled the trails they once tread proud,
Leaving the weary under a darkened cloud.

The mighty Gorilla, with hands like stone,
Labored long, yet felt alone.
The sleek Cheetah, once fast as air,
Now dragged her feet in deep despair.

Then chaos struck, the jungle's throne fell,
The Lions deposed, their kingdom a shell.
The young Hyenas, teeth sharp, eyes cold,
Seized the riches with guns and gold.

No law, no love, no justice found,
As the weak were trampled on bloodied ground.
Teenage warriors, barely grown,
Claimed the jungle as their own.

In the heart of this turmoil, the Parrot cried,
"What is justice, where does it hide?
We feast on the scraps of what once was ours,
While darkness devours the light of the stars."

An hour too late, the tragedy struck,
Five lives lost to cruel, fickle luck.
The Antelope wept as news spread wide,
The jungle mourned, its hope denied.

The Cafeteria Tree, once lush with fruit,
Stood barren now, its roots destitute.
Corn spilled out, oil dripped dry,
While the Monkey and Rabbit watched with a sigh.

The Elephant spoke with a rumble deep,
"Why do my friends no longer keep
The promises made, the kindness shared?
Have they forgotten the love we declared?"

The Crocodile rested by the river's edge,
"I gave them shelter, I gave my pledge.
Yet now they fight for the bread I bring,
And see me as a foe, not a king."

But amidst the gloom, a flicker grew,
A Firefly's light, humble yet true.
Her voice was soft, yet her words were bold,
"Yesterday's darkness need not take hold."

"Beasts of the jungle, come near, unite,
Let our shadows fade in this humble light.
The matchstick burns, a beacon bright,
Unmatched by chaos, unrivaled by night."

The animals gathered, their gazes raised,
As the tiny Firefly's light blazed.
Together they stood, paw in claw,
Rebuilding the jungle with hope and awe.

For amidst the chaos, the lesson clear,
It's love and unity that conquer fear.
And though the jungle bore scars of pain,
Its heart beat strong with life again.

So remember the tale of the jungle's plight,
Where shadows fell but rose the light.
A story of beasts, of loss, of gain,
Of sparks that endure through storm and rain.

End

Don't miss out!

Visit the website below and you can sign up to receive emails whenever Cornelius Wambi Gulere publishes a new book. There's no charge and no obligation.

https://books2read.com/r/B-A-LESJD-WVDZF

BOOKS 2 READ

Connecting independent readers to independent writers.

Did you love *I Died, I Am Dead, I Die*? Then you should read *The Narrow Gate: Nature's Storms*[1] by Cornelius Wambi Gulere!

"*The door to the Kingdom is not found in the height of pride, but in the depth of humility. The road to resurrection is paved not with self-righteousness, but with repentance.*"

In this powerful poetry anthology, Presby. Cornelius Wambi Gulere masterfully weaves together Orthodox theology, cultural wisdom, and poetic meditation to create a liturgical guide for all who seek to journey through the Great Fast with sincerity and depth. Through allegory, fable, riddles, and long-form poetry, this collection offers a soulful reflection on repentance, divine mercy, and the transformative power of humility.

---

1. https://books2read.com/u/bWkx9q

2. https://books2read.com/u/bWkx9q

A must-read for anyone seeking a deeper connection to the Orthodox journey of faith, this anthology calls us to kneel in humility, rise in love, and embrace the joy of reconciliation.

Read more at https://www.facebook.com/cornelius.wambigulere.1.

Also by Cornelius Wambi Gulere

I Died, I Am Dead, I Die
The Narrow Gate: Nature's Storms
The Human Brain

Watch for more at https://www.facebook.com/
cornelius.wambigulere.1.

About the Author

The Weaver of Words, Wisdom, and Wonder

Dr. Cornelius Wambi Gulere is a literary craftsman whose work spans the rich terrains of poetry, storytelling, riddles, and academic scholarship. A poet by heart, a storyteller by tradition, and a scholar by discipline, his writings pulse with the rhythm of African oral heritage, the depth of theological inquiry, and the urgency of contemporary discourse. Whether capturing the whispers of ancestral voices in riddles, sculpting narratives that bridge past and future, or illuminating linguistic treasures in academic tomes, he is a literary force whose ink never dries.

Born in Nsinze, Uganda, and nurtured by the echoes of Orthodox chants and the cadence of Lusoga folklore, Dr. Gulere's literary journey has been a dynamic fusion of faith, culture, and scholarship. His Ph.D. research at Makerere University explored **Riddles and Riddling in Lusoga Language and Culture**, unearthing the aesthetic, philosophical, and didactic **riddle performance theory** showing power of oral traditions. This passion has fueled his work in education, translation, and creative writing, bringing indigenous storytelling to new generations.

An accomplished author and editor, his works appear in various literary anthologies, online platforms, and academic journals. He has been instrumental in the **African Storybook Project**, curating and translating children's literature into Lusoga and over 60 other languages. His seminal work, the *Eibwanio Fountain Lusoga–English Dictionary*, remains a cornerstone of language preservation; *A Very Mall Man,* his classic children's story has been read worldwide in over 100 languages.

Beyond the page, Dr. Gulere is a **priest, educator, and community advocate**, blending theological depth with literary brilliance. Whether leading worship at St. Sophia Orthodox Parish or pioneering linguistic preservation efforts, he remains committed to the transformative power of words—written, spoken, and lived.

In print or online, in riddles or reflections, in the classroom or the pulpit, **Cornelius Wambi Gulere writes not just for today, but for generations yet to come.**

Explore his works, unravel his riddles, and step into the story.

Read more at https://www.facebook.com/cornelius.wambigulere.1.

About the Publisher

I was Hungry!

Dear Reader,

This collection was born out of moments both joyful and trying, drawing from the lives of those who, in their silent strength, teach us what it means to endure. Each poem reflects a story—a life, a struggle, a victory—woven together to remind us of the interconnectedness of our humanity.

As you turn these pages, you will walk beside a priest bearing the silent cross of service, a mother navigating the many paths of love, and a father whose unseen pillar supports generations. You will witness the beauty of unity, the pain of loss, and the triumph of grace.

Let these words be a mirror to your own journey, a comfort in times of doubt, and a call to celebrate the interconnectedness of lives that surrounds us. In every verse, may you find a thread that resonates, that binds, and that inspires.

Every page of this anthology is woven with stories of resilience, faith, and the boundless strength of the human spirit. But its impact reaches beyond these words. By purchasing this book, you are becoming part of a greater story—one of hope, opportunity, and transformation. This is what **Beads of Love** is.

All proceeds from the sale of this anthology will go directly to supporting education and empowering mothers striving to keep their children in school. Your contribution will help provide the resources they need to ensure that education is not just a routine, but a rewarding journey that nurtures young minds to grow into capable, compassionate, and useful citizens.

Through your support, we are building a bridge for those who dream of a brighter future but face significant challenges. Together, we can transform lives, one child, one mother, one family at a time. Thank you for being part of this mission.

Your donation is received with gratitude on:

Venmo: Cornelius-Gulere
+1 617 444 6900